Totally Uncool

Totally Uncool

by Janice Levy
illustrated by Chris Monroe

Carolrhoda Books, Inc./Minneapolis

Dad's new girlfriend is weird.
Totally uncool.

She plays the tuba.
Reads poems that don't rhyme.
Falls asleep sitting up.

Dad calls her Sweet Potato.
I don't call her anything.

She doesn't play soccer.
Or work out in a gym.
Video games? She hasn't a clue.

Sweet Potato would never think of ice skating.
Or horseback riding.
Shooting hoops? I don't think so.

She doesn't bake cookies.
Her kitchen floor is too shiny.
Mostly everything she eats is green.

Sweet Potato wears sneakers with skirts.
And sometimes backwards baseball caps.

Her hair is porcupiny.

She sings opera to her goldfish.
Hangs upside down to relax.
Forgets the answers to riddles.

She speaks Spanish to her neighbors.

Baby talk to my dad.

Japanese to her plants.

And mish-mosh to me.

Scary movies give her nightmares.
Cats make her sneeze.
Loud music clogs her ears.

Sweet Potato is weird. Totally uncool.
Still, out of all the girlfriends,
she's lasted the longest....

She listens to me without the TV on.
Keeps my secrets secret.
Never interrupts me when I stutter.

She tests me on my spelling words.
Lets me slam doors when things aren't fair.
She never calls me stupid.

At school plays, Dad's new girlfriend
claps the loudest.

She waits (and waits) at the finish line.

She helped me with my Halloween costume.
It won First Prize.
Nobody else came as Broccoli.

She doesn't call my stuff "junk."
Or touch it without asking first.
I can make messes if they're just on me.

If I'm grouchy, Dad's new girlfriend
doesn't try to make me laugh.
Or ask a zillion questions.
She lets me be quiet.

She doesn't yell when I forget things.
Or drop things.
Well, maybe just a little.

She takes my side when I get in a fight.
She rubs away my headaches.
She says it's okay to cry.

She doesn't order me around.
Or make me do things "just because."
She doesn't stay mad forever.

Her real name is Elizabeth.
Maybe there's hope for her yet.

To Rick, with all my love
—J. L.

To Mickey
—C. M.

Carolrhoda Books, Inc., c/o The Lerner Publishing Group
241 First Avenue North, Minneapolis, MN 55401 U.S.A.

Website address: www.lernerbooks.com

Library of Congress Cataloging-in-Publication Data

Levy, Janice.
Totally uncool / by Janice Levy : illustrated
by Chris Monroe.
p.   cm.
Summary: As she describes all the things that are "uncool" about
her father's latest girlfriend, a young girl begins to admit that
there are some things she likes about her.
ISBN 1-57505-306-3
[1. Single-parent family—Fiction. 2. Interpersonal relations—
Fiction. 3. Fathers and daughters—Fiction.]
I. Monroe, Chris, ill. II. Title.
PZ7.L5832To   1999
[E]—dc21   98-6900

Manufactured in the United States of America
1 2 3 4 5 6 - JR - 04 03 02 01 00 99